Ben's Bean

Ben's Bean

PAT MOON

Illustrated by
TIM ARCHBOLD

ORCHARD BOOKS

For Ben - at last.
Only ten years late!
P.M.

ORCHARD BOOKS
96 Leonard Street, London EC2A 4RH
Orchard Books Australia
14 Mars Road, Lane Cove NSW 2066
1 85213 825 4 (hardback)
1 85213 820 3 (paperback)
Text © Pat Moon 1995
Illustrations © Tim Archbold 1995
First published in Great Britain in 1995
First paperback publication 1996
The right of Pat Moon to be identified as the Author
and Tim Archbold as the Illustrator of this Work
has been asserted by them in accordance with the
Copyright, Designs and Patents Act, 1988.
A CIP catalogue record for this book is available
from the British Library.
Printed in Great Britain

Contents

1

Wait and See

"Don't be daft!" said Clare, as her brother Ben picked up the bean from the pavement. "Of course it's not magic."

"It COULD be," said Ben. "Look."

It was large and pale green with dark-green streaks.

"It's just an ordinary old bean," said Clare. "There's no such thing as magic beans."

"There is in *Jack and the Beanstalk*," said Ben.

"That's just a silly fairy-tale," said Clare. "It's not true."

Beans don't get dropped on pavements, thought Ben. This IS magic. You wait and see.

As soon as he got home, he planted it in the flowerbed beneath his bedroom window.

"Bet you it's not magic, " said Clare. "Bet you a million pounds."

Ben checked his bean eleven times before bedtime. It will probably shoot up during the night, he told himself.

As soon as he woke, he rushed to the window and saw – nothing but a cloudy sky.

"You owe me a million pounds," said Clare at breakfast.

"It hasn't had long enough yet," said Ben.

But there was nothing to see when he got home from school either. Or the next day. Or the next week. He forgot about his bean.

Then one night Ben couldn't sleep. Even with his window wide open his room was stuffy. His tongue felt like a piece of old carpet. He needed a drink. A long, cool drink. The more he thought about it, the more furry his tongue seemed to grow. He climbed out of bed. The house was dark and silent, and he felt his way down the stairs to the kitchen. Pale moonlight had turned it into a cave of eerie shadows. Quickly, Ben grabbed a cup, opened the fridge, poured out some lemonade and gulped greedily. Dee-licious. He turned to pour another. And froze.

There was something at the window. Something large and crawling. Crawling slowly on long, thin legs, like a giant stick insect. Ben stood as still as a statue while the shadow of the crawling thing crept over the worktops. He wanted to yell. He wanted to run. But he couldn't.

Can it see me? What if I move? Will it smash through and grab me?

It covered the window now, scratching and clawing as if it were trying to get at him.

At that moment, the moon slipped from behind a cloud, spotlighting the crawling thing. Ben stared, gasped and stepped forward.

"Not a giant insect!" he breathed. "A plant! It's a plant!"

He rushed closer. Claw-like leaves

unfurled from bent sidestalks, looking exactly like a giant, crawling creature. But this was where he had planted his bean. His bean was GROWING!

He had to get outside. He ran to the back door and turned the key. But the bolt wouldn't budge. He ran to the front door, unlocked it and dashed round through the side gate into the back garden. And there it was. HIS beanstalk – shooting upwards.

Ben jumped on to a pair of sideshoots, grabbing a higher pair. He didn't have to climb. The plant was climbing for him.

Up, up, up he went, past his bedroom window, leaving his house, and Mum and Dad and Clare, far behind.

The house shrank and disappeared into the blackness.

Suddenly, he didn't want to go.

But the plant was growing faster and faster. It was too late.

He didn't dare move. He remembered the giant in the storybook. That horrible, hairy face. And those terrible teeth. Perhaps the giant was waiting for him. Any minute now a huge hand would swoop from the darkness, snatch him up and those terrible teeth would bite his head off. He shivered and shut his eyes. Whatever happened next, he didn't want to see it. The air rushed past him, flapping his pyjamas.

Then the rushing slowed. The plant stopped. Slowly, Ben opened his eyes.

And stared. Below was a giant flowerbed. He was in a huge, sunny garden surrounded by a towering fence. Everything was giant-sized. In the distance stood a giant house.

He started to clamber down.
Something brushed against his face.
He wiped it away. But it clung to his
fingers.

"Ugh," he grunted when he saw he
was covered with spider's web. Then
he saw the spider. The size of a plate.
Furry. Brown and orange. Black
beady eyes glinting, fangs twitching,

it scuttled towards him. This time Ben yelled. He tore himself away and ran and ran. With a desperate look behind him, he threw himself onto the grass, heaving.

At last he stopped shaking.

"I'm going home. Now!" he said, getting up.

Then, everything went black.

"Got you!" said a voice.

2

Big Problems

A shaft of light beamed down. He
was trapped inside a giant flowerpot.
He glimpsed a huge eye trying to peer
in. The pot tipped and an enormous
hand lifted him into the sky. Then
darkness again as the zip of a bag
whizzed shut above him. He swung

and bounced as the bag's owner ran shouting, "Look what I've got!"

"In here!" shouted another voice. "In the kitchen."

PLEASE, thought Ben, don't eat me!

Then a different voice, so loud that it made Ben's ears tingle.

"Let's see what you've got then."

The zip whizzed again and light

flooded in. Ben saw a giant hand
reach down. Then he saw the face.

An enormous face with freckles, long
blonde plaits and blue eyes looking
down at him. He stared up at the
giant girl, terrified.

Suddenly, the girl seemed to change
her mind.

"Oh dear, it must have escaped – the little frog I caught. What a shame."

The zip whizzed shut once more and it was dark again. As the girl skipped away, through a split in the bag Ben glimpsed two giant, booted feet.

If those trod on me, he thought, they wouldn't even notice.

The bouncing stopped. The zip whizzed. "You can come out now," said the girl.

Blinking, Ben crawled into the light. The giant girl crouched before him with a toy tennis racquet half raised, ready to swipe. Just as if he were a poisonous pest.

"You'd better not try anything," she said, "or I'll take you straight down to my dad. Then you'll be for it."

Dinner probably, Ben couldn't help thinking.

They studied one another. The girl
wore shorts and a T-shirt. Ben barely
reached her knee.

"Are you anything to do with Jack?" she asked.

He shook his head.

"But you're human, aren't you?" she accused, squinting at him.

He nodded.

"I'm Ada. I'm six and a quarter. What's your name?"

"Ben," said Ben.

She leaned forward.

"You're very tiny," she said.

"Yeah ... well, you're very big," said Ben.

She grinned. "Oh, look at your tiny little hands and toes! And your little suit! You're sweet!"

"I'm not!" said Ben. "And they're pyjamas."

She laughed and started to stroke his hair and move his arms up and down and examine his pyjamas. He wanted to push her away and shout, "Leave off, will you!" But she was so BIG. He backed away and started to look around.

There was a vast bed with a huge fluffy blue rabbit on the pillow. A doll's pram holding a baby doll (larger than himself) stood before a looming chest of drawers. Enormous pens and pencils and sheets of paper lay on the floor.

Ada followed, watching closely. Ben was more interested in her toys. That

pram would make a brilliant go-cart if he could steer it. And what about that giant slide?

"You ought to be grateful to me," said Ada. "I've just saved your life. And you haven't even said thank you."

She stood, arms folded, slowly tapping the racquet against her shoulder.

"Thank you," said Ben quickly. "Thank you very much. Thank you very much indeed."

"That's better," she said.

But Ben didn't feel very safe. He knew she could squash him flat. She could throw him across the room. She might pull his arms and legs off. Ada could do anything she liked with him. He was on his own.

"Please," said Ben, "could you take me back to the garden? I'd like to go home now."

She ignored him, opening up a large
box and laying out clothes on the
floor. Then she fetched some dolls
and sat them in a circle. She picked
out a pair of stripy trousers, a green
fluffy jumper and a pair of yellow
knitted bootees.

"Perfect," she said.

Before he knew it, Ben was grabbed
and thrown across her knee. She
started to unbutton his pyjama top.

"Get off!" he yelled, kicking and wriggling off her lap. "I'm not a doll!"

"Come here at once!" she demanded. "Or I'll scream so loud my daddy will come running and ..."

He didn't wait for the rest. He ran. Dodging and darting as she stamped behind him. He dived for the chest of drawers and wriggled under it just as Ada made a grab. He saw her chubby fingers grasping as he crawled backwards. Her face squinted in at him.

"All right," she said sweetly. "We'll play something else. I'll let you choose."

Silence.

"OK. Please yourself," she said, disappearing. "Stay there if you like. You can make friends with the big black spider that lives at the back."

Ben was out before you could say "web".

3

Nothing but Trouble

"All right," agreed Ben grumpily. "I'll play on the slide. But no dressing up."

Ada smiled triumphantly.

He whizzed down on Ada's lap.

He whizzed down by himself.

But somehow he couldn't really enjoy it. He kept remembering that he was at the mercy of a six-year-old giant.

"I have to go home now," he said, smiling politely.

"It's not allowed," said Ada. "All human beings have to be reported."

"What happens then?" asked Ben.

Ada thought hard. "They're never seen again."

"Take me back and you'll never see ME again," said Ben. "Promise."

"Daddy says humans are nothing but trouble. Like that nasty Jack."

"He wasn't nasty," said Ben before he could stop himself. "He was brave! He killed the fierce, ugly, horrible giant!"

"He wasn't brave!" yelled Ada. "And I don't like you any more!"

Ben could see now that it was a big mistake to boast about killing giants with someone four times bigger than you.

"I've got a book about it," said Ben. "It calls him BRAVE Jack."

"Right – I'll show you!" cried Ada, snatching him up.

Next minute he was bouncing along in the dark again as Ada thumped down the stairs with her bag.

He hardly dared look when she lifted him out. But there were no giants.

Just a huge sitting room with giant
furniture. She held him up.

"You're very lucky, you know that?
I could have taken you straight to my
dad."

He dangled helplessly.

"Now, I'm going to trust you. But
any tricks - and that's it!"

"I can be trusted," said Ben. "Just
don't treat me like a toy. I'm a boy."

"OK," Ada shrugged.

She put him on to the sideboard next to a vase of flowers the size of a small tree.

"Right," said Ada importantly. "See him?" She pointed to a framed photo on the sideboard. It showed an old man with a droopy white moustache sitting in a sunny garden and smiling from under an old straw hat.

"That's who Jack killed," she announced.

"You sure?" asked Ben. The old man didn't look fierce or ugly. He looked rather friendly.

"Of course I'm sure. He was my daddy's great-grandad Albert. He wasn't horrible or – What's the matter?"

Ben, open-mouthed, stared at the door. It was opening. He darted behind the vase. Only just in time.

"Ada? You haven't seen my small scissors, have you? I can't find them anywhere."

"I think I saw them over there, Mummy," he heard Ada answer.

"No, look! There they are," said Ada's mum. "On the sideboard.

Next to the vase."

Heart pounding, Ben pressed himself against the vase as heavy footsteps thumped towards him.

"Here you are, Mummy," Ada said.

"Thank you, Ada."

Ada's mum was so close, if Ben stretched out his hand, he could touch her. She was enormous. His heart was pumping fit to burst.

The footsteps retreated. He let out the breath he hadn't known he was holding. PHEW! Carefully, he peeped out.

"Wait!" screamed Ada.

But it was too late.

He'd been seen.

Sniffing the air in his direction stood a cat. Black. As big as a panther. Its yellow eyes fixed on to him.

Everything happened at once.

Ada grabbed.

The cat leapt.

The vase went flying.

Ben went skidding and sailed through the air.

Ada screamed.

The room spun.

Ada's mum shouted.

Something crashed.

And then he was upside-down.

"What's that behind your back, Ada?" demanded her mum.

"Just my doll," lied Ada.

"Now, Ada," said her mum, "I saw him. Give him to me, please. I've shut Blackie out."

"Sorry, Ben," said Ada.

She really did sound sorry. As if she knew what was waiting for him. His mouth went dry.

"A human child," said Ada's mum. "Why didn't you tell us, Ada? You know the rules."

"He's my friend," said Ada. "I was worried about him."

"We'll see what your father has to say about that," said Ada's mum. "Come along."

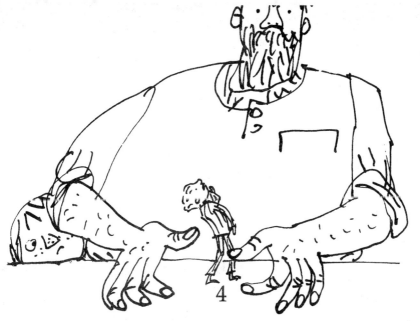

4

Is He Going to Eat Me?

Ben stood before the giant on the giant table in the giant kitchen. The giant's hands, like a pair of five-legged monsters on guard, lay one on either side of him.

The giant peered down at Ben.

"Put the kettle on, Dora," he said to Ada's mum.

I'm going to be boiled, thought Ben.

"Now," growled the giant, "you'd better tell me the truth. Because if you don't - I'll – I'll – I'll get really angry!"

Ben started to tremble. He couldn't help it.

"Oh, poor little thing," said Ada's mum, picking him up. "Don't frighten him so, George."

Then to Ben she said, "All right now, love?"

"Is he going to eat me?" whispered Ben.

"Eat you?" said Ada's mum.

"Eat you?" roared the giant.

"Ugh!" said Ada, making a face.

"Yes, you know, like the giant wanted to eat Jack."

"No," glared George. "We don't know. Why don't you tell us?"

"Well," said Ben, shaking, "in my book, it says that Jack climbs a beanstalk and comes to a great big house. When the giant's wife hears the giant, she says, 'Quick, hide in the oven or he'll eat you.' But the giant can smell him and says,

> 'FEE FI FO FUM,
> I SMELL THE BLOOD OF AN
> ENGLISHMAN.
> BE HE ALIVE OR BE HE DEAD,
> I'LL GRIND HIS BONES TO
> MAKE MY BREAD'."

The giant began to chuckle. The chuckle grew into a laugh. He threw back his head and shook with such laughter that it made Ben's head vibrate. Ada was giggling and her mum's lap was shaking too.

"I've never heard anything like it!" he chuckled. "What was that again? FEE FI FO FUM? I must remember that. FEE FI FO FUM!"

"Go on, go on, " cried Ada, hopping up and down. "What happened next?"

So he told them. How the giant fell asleep and Jack crept out and stole the gold. How he went back again and again, for the magic hen and the singing harp. How the giant had chased him. How Jack had chopped down the beanstalk. How the giant had fallen down – dead.

But no one was laughing now.

"But it's only a story," said Ben, uncomfortably.

"Oh no, it isn't," said George the giant. "It happened all right. But not like that. Wait there."

He went away and returned with a piece of paper which he spread on the table. It was old and creased, covered in large print. It had been cut from a giant newspaper.

"Here, Dora," he said. "You read it for us."

Ada's mum began to read.

TRAGIC DEATH OF PENSIONER

Retired postman, Mr. Albert Little plunged to his death yesterday trying to stop a thief from taking off with his singing harp. His wife, Mrs. Lily Little, was too upset to talk. Neighbours say that Mr Little had made friends with a human youth by the name of Jack, who had climbed into Mr Little's garden by beanstalk. Their prize hen and life savings are also missing. Mr Little was killed when the human Jack chopped down the beanstalk.

Readers are reminded to watch for stray beanstalks and report all sightings of humans straight away.

"He was a nice old man," added Ada's mum sadly. "They'd been kind to Jack – treated him like a son. Jack was nothing but a thief and a murderer."

"So there really was a Jack," said Ben. "But I don't understand – it was hundreds of years ago."

"Oh, time's different here," said Ada's mum. "Everything here is bigger. Why, it would take twenty or

more of your years to make one of
ours. Now, the kettle's boiled. I'll
make some tea."

She stood Ben on the table.

"I'm very sorry!" Ben shouted up to
George. "About what Jack did. I
won't steal your gold. Honest!"

"Well," said George. "What do you
say, Ada?"

"He's nice," said Ada.

"He IS just a little 'un," said George.

"I think we can trust this one. Not all humans are bad."

"Can we keep him, then, Mum?" said Ada. "Can he stay now?"

"Of course he can't," said Dora, pouring the tea. "He's got a home of his own, just like you, and a mum and dad – wondering where he is, I expect."

Ben had forgotten about Mum and Dad. Were they still asleep?

"I've put it in a thimble for you, love." Dora smiled as she handed Ben his tea.

"Drink up, Ben," said George. "I think it's time you went home."

George lifted Ben up, up, up and slid him into his shirt pocket.

"Hold on tight, Ben," he said.

The ground seemed miles off as George strode out to the beanstalk.

"I'd better take him down, Dora," he said.

"Goodbye, Ben," called Ada. "Come back again."

As George stepped on to the stalk, the ground opened and Ben glimpsed the darkness below.

"Is this it Ben? Is this your house?"

Ben shook himself awake. Yes. There was his window. There was his bed. Everything just as he had left it.

George lowered him in.

"Thanks," said Ben.

"You hop into bed now," said George. "Bye, little 'un."

Ben waved, but as George's giant feet climbed upwards, the plant shimmered and slowly disappeared until Ben was staring at an empty sky.

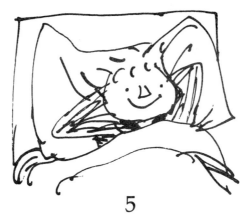

5

The Great Mysteries

Ben woke. What a brilliant dream. The best ever. He lay there thinking about it.

The door opened slowly and Clare peeped in.

"About time. Awake at last," she said. "You've missed all the excitement. You slept through it all. You'll never guess what's happened – not in a zillion years."

"Go on then, what?" said Ben.

"We've been burgled!" she said.

"Cor," said Ben. "What did they take, then?"

"Nothing," said Clare. "That's one of the great mysteries. Nothing's gone at all."

"How d'you know we've been burgled then?"

"They left the front door wide open – all night. Anyone could have walked in. They'd unlocked the back door too, though the bolt was still on, and the side gate was open ... "

Clare was pleased to see that Ben's eyes seemed to be popping out of his head.

"... but the greatest mystery of all is – they dug a huge hole in the flowerbed. Just where you'd planted your daft bean."

"What for?" croaked Ben.

"That's the mystery," said Clare. "No one knows. The police are here, investigating. Dad's talking to them now."

"Clare! Can you come down for a moment?" Dad's voice called up the stairs.

"Coming," replied Clare.

Ben rushed to the window. Where'd he planted his bean there was a huge, earthy hole with flowers lying around it. Dollops of earth covered the path and there on his window-ledge was a sprinkling of soil, just as if an enormous plant had been pulled up. He wiped it off with one of his socks.

Someone was coming up the stairs. In walked Dad, followed by Mum and a policeman.

"PC Parker here wants to ask you a few questions about our break-in, Ben," said Dad. "Just in case you saw or heard anything."

PC Parker went to the window and looked down.

"Now, Ben," he said. "Was your window open all night?"

Ben nodded.

"And did you hear anything? Noises, voices, anything like that?"

Ben shook his head as PC Parker made jottings in a notebook.

"Just one more thing, Ben," he said. "We think the intruder may have helped himself to some lemonade. There was a cup and a bottle left out and your mum says she definitely cleared everything away last night. No one else knows anything about it. We can check them for fingerprints once we are sure that it was no one in the family. Did YOU have a drink last night?"

"I might have done," said Ben. "I was very thirsty."

"Can you remember when that was?" asked the policeman.

"Sorry," said Ben.

"Well, thanks, Ben, " said PC Parker, shutting his notebook. He and Mum left the room.

"I just can't understand it," said Ben's dad as he peered out of the window again. "Who would want to dig a hole in our flowerbed? It beats me, it really does. Well, one thing's for sure, I won't forget today in a hurry."

No, thought Ben, neither will I.

There was something else he wouldn't forget in a hurry.

"Hey, Clare!" he shouted down over the banisters. "You owe me a million pounds!"